Cú Chulainn

A FAMILY TIME FABLES BOOK

Wayne Kearns

CÚ CHULAINN BY WAYNE KEARNS

Dedication

For Gary, Yasmine, Scott, Ben, Evan and Dylan -
the inspirations for this book - and for all boys and girls
brave enough to follow their dreams.

SETANTA WAS A YOUNG SIX year old boy who loved to swim and hunt and fish and fight and play hurling with his father and friends.

The greatest wish Setanta had was to become one of the Red Branch Knights – the strongest and most skilful warriors in the land.

5

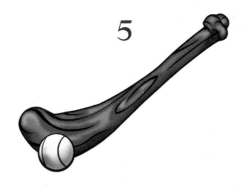

Every night before going to sleep, Setanta asked his parents if he could go to Emhain Macha to meet his uncle King Connor who was the leader of the Red Branch Knights, and ask him to join.

They knew that Setanta was a very special boy with many talents but they told him that he was too young and would have to wait until he was older and bigger.

6

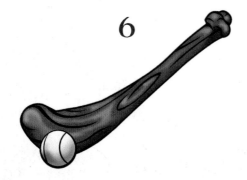

Early one morning, Setanta decided to go on an adventure. He left his house and set out to reach Emhain Macha by himself. He travelled over mountains, through forests and across rivers.

The only thing he carried with him was his sliotar and his hurley.

As he walked through the strange countryside, he was a little scared – but he carried on walking.

9

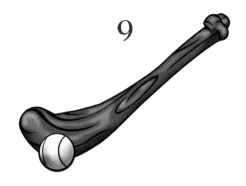

Finally, after a long walk, Setanta reached Emhain Macha.

He saw a large group of older boys playing hurling outside the castle. Setanta was tired after his long journey but he asked could he join the game.

11

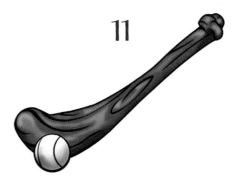

Setanta was younger and smaller than the other boys but he was a better player than them all. Soon, the other boys became angry that they were losing and began to shout and be rough.

King Connor was sitting inside his castle and heard the loud noises. He looked out and saw Setanta winning the game.

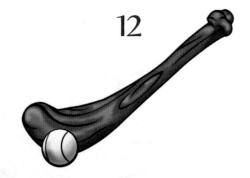

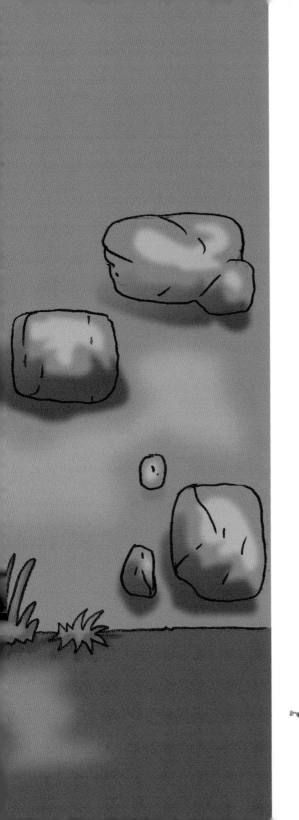

King Connor wanted to know who this new boy was that was so good at hurling.

He came outside and asked Setanta his name. Setanta told him that he was the King's nephew and that he had travelled all this way to become a Red Branch Knight.

15

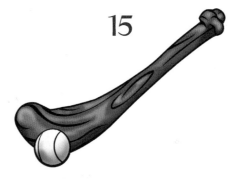

King Connor was surprised by the story and smiled at the idea of someone so small wanting to become a Knight.

He brought Setanta into the castle to meet some of the Red Branch Knights but they laughed when they heard Setanta's dream, because he was so young.

Seeing how tired he was after his long journey, King Connor sent Setanta to have some food and explore the castle.

Setanta set off on his new adventure around the castle and had lots of fun exploring and looking at all of the rooms and everything in them.

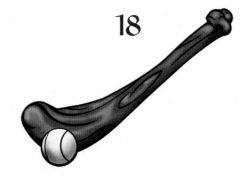

On the same day, a large feast was taking place nearby at the fort of Culann the Blacksmith.

King Connor invited Setanta to come and join the party. Setanta was having such a good time exploring the castle, that he told the King that he would follow everyone to the feast later.

21

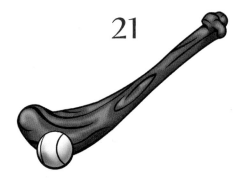

Everyone was having a great time at Culann's fort.

King Connor met many friends when he got there and forgot to tell Culann that Setanta would be joining them later.

Culann thought that everyone had arrived at the party and closed the gates.

He placed his fiercest and biggest hound at the entrance to guard the fort.

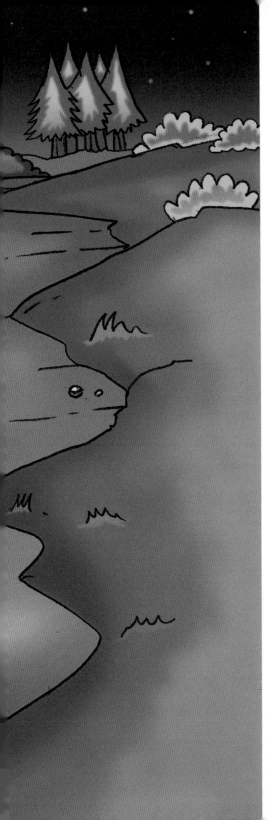

When he finished exploring the castle, Setanta picked up his sliotar and hurley and left the castle to join everyone at the feast at Culann's fort.

The day had passed really quickly and night had begun to fall.

As he got close to the fort, Setanta heard a loud and scary growling noise and saw the fierce hound.

25

The hound jumped up to attack Setanta, but Setanta acted quickly and hit the sliotar towards the hound with his hurley in order to stop him.

The sliotar hit the big scary hound and killed him.

26

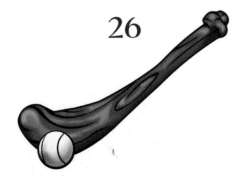

The people inside the fort heard the hound barking and howling and came outside to investigate.

They were surprised to see the hound was dead and wondered who this small boy was that was standing beside it.

The blacksmith Culann was very upset that his biggest and fiercest hound was dead.

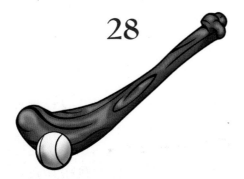

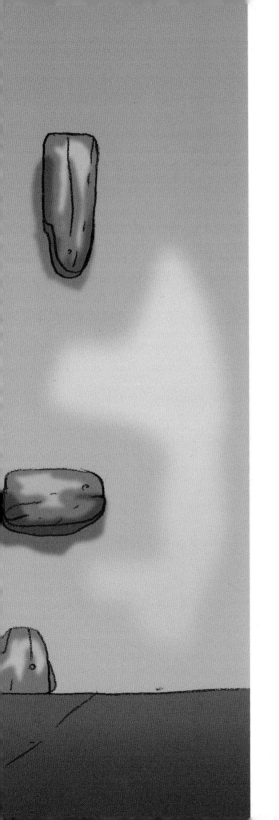

Culann and King Connor were very unhappy and angry that they no longer had a hound to help guard the blacksmith's fort.

Culann said that it would take one year to train another hound to be good at guarding.

Setanta wanted to show that he was very sorry and offered to guard Culann's fort for a year while the new hound was being trained.

31

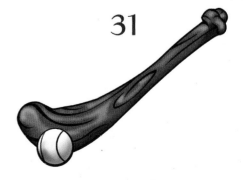

Culann understood that Setanta was sorry and saw that he was a very brave boy.

For the year that Setanta guarded the fort, his name was changed to Cú Chulainn - meaning Culann's hound.

Even though Setanta grew up to join the Red Branch Knights and be one of their greatest warriors, he was always known as Cú Chulainn.

33

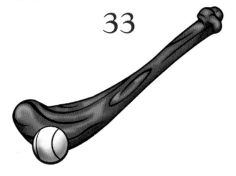

Printed in Great Britain
by Amazon